ALL ABOARD at SILVER STREET FARM

ALL ABOARD at SILVER STREET FARM

NICOLA DAVIES
illustrated by Katharine McEwen

First published 2011 by Walker Books Ltd
87 Vauxhall Walk, London SE11 5HJ

2 4 6 8 10 9 7 5 3

This book has been typeset in Stempel Schneidler and Cows

Printed and bound in Great Britain
by Clays Ltd, St Ives plc

British Library Cataloguing in Publication Data:
a catalogue record for this book is available from the British Library

ISBN 978-1-4063-2305-4

www.walker.co.uk

For Joseph and Gabriel,
wrens on the wardrobe
and "terriere derrière".

A MAP OF
SILVER STREET FARM
Main gate
FLORA'S OFFICE + FLAT
FLORA'S VAN
Goats
Sheep
gate
Duck House
CANAL
N

Pigs
fence
DAIRY
Yard for Pigs
Out-house
out-house
Turkeys
Chicken Roost
Pen
Turkey Pen
Old metal bridge

Chapter One

It was the hottest summer anyone in Lonchester could remember. The grass in the parks turned brown and police went on patrol in short-sleeved shirts. Hosepipes were banned. Strangers greeted one another in the street, looking up at the clear blue sky and saying, "Phew! Another scorcher!"

At Silver Street City Farm, the pigs – Mrs Fattybot, Mojo and their piglets – were getting sunburned, and it was decided that they should have a mud bath to keep them cool.

So that was why, on the first afternoon of the summer holidays, Meera, Karl and Gemma, the three children who had started Silver Street, were struggling across the farmyard with big buckets, brimful of water.

"These last three should do it," panted Karl.

"Good job. My arms are almost dropping off," complained Gemma.

"I hope the pigs appreciate all this work!" said Meera.

The pigs lived in solid brick and concrete sties, but they could also be let out into a big fenced pen to root around amongst the weeds and scrubby bushes. The children emptied their buckets into the hollow scrape that Karl had made in the middle of this pen with a

shovel and Karl tested the spot with his boot; it disappeared up to the ankle in liquid mud.

"Perfect!" he said. "Now, let's see if they like it."

"Well, if *they* don't," Meera laughed, "Gemma and me are getting in there to cool off!"

Karl opened the gates to the two sties and a gang of half-grown piglets, ginger with big black spots, shot out of each one. They ran around, chasing each other and splashing in the wallow, snorting and blowing, sending mud in all directions.

"Aw!" said Meera. "They're getting so covered in mud you can't see their black spots."

"That's the idea, Meera," Karl replied. "The mud is like suntan lotion, it stops them getting burned."

"Maybe I'll try putting some mud on the

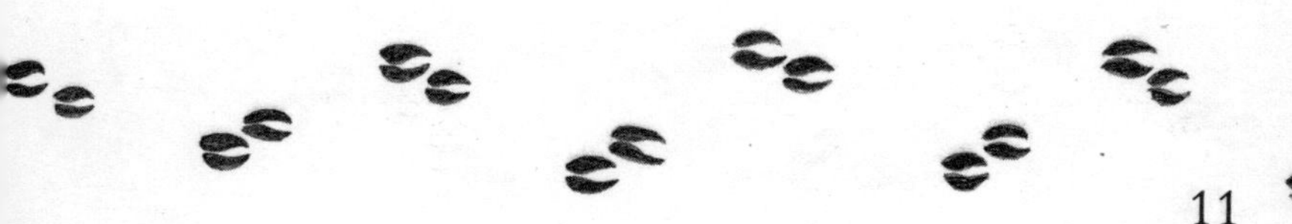

end of my nose," grinned Gemma. "It might stop me getting any more freckles!"

Deep snorts and grunts came from inside the sties. The mummy pigs were getting up.

Mojo was out first, her huge, round body balanced over her neat little trotters, like an overstuffed sofa on antique legs. She took a deep breath, sniffing the mud, and then rushed into the mudbath.

The second sow, Mrs Fattybot, was never an early riser. But Mojo's sigh must have told her that she was missing out on something good. She emerged from the sty, ears flapping, as if to say "What's going on?", then barged Mojo to one side and plonked herself down in the lovely, sloppy centre of the bath, as if it was the *least* that a pig of her quality could expect. The children smiled at each other.

"She looks like she's expecting us to bring her cocktails!" said Meera.

"I know!" said Karl, shaking his head and laughing.

"C'mon guys," said Gemma. "No slacking! All the *other* animals need water now!"

The three friends lugged full buckets about the farm, laughing and joking and splashing each other to keep cool. The whole of the summer holidays stretched out in front of them, full of days like this. Although Flora, the farm manager, did most of the work on the farm, helping out was still what they all loved doing best in all the world.

In spite of their high spirits, the children couldn't ignore the fact that some of the Silver Street animals were not quite so happy. The chickens had given up scratching for worms and just hung about in the shade under their pen, looking bored. The turkeys spent all day panting and dust-bathing, and although the ducks still swam in the canal, the water was green and icky. There wasn't a scrap of grass growing in any of the pens; the heat had shrivelled it up weeks ago. So the goats and sheep had no fresh greens to eat, only hay and the muesli-like food that came in sacks. The goats didn't seem to mind this too much, but the sheep were truly fed up.

When the children arrived at the ewes' pen, Bobo and Bitzi and their four lambs were crammed together in the shade of a small bush, the only patch of shelter from the sun.

"Oh, dear!" said Gemma. "They look way too hot!"

Reluctantly, the sheep left the shade to get

their hay and water. The ewes let the children scratch their woolly heads, and one of the lambs nibbled gently at Meera's leg.

Meera giggled. "All right," she said. "You don't have to tickle me. We'll see if we can find some more shade for you."

Gemma nodded.

"And some fresh grass to eat," Karl added quietly to himself as they crossed the yard to refill their buckets.

Flora MacDonald sat at her desk in the Silver Street Farm office, her dark hair even curlier than usual with sheer worry. She was looking at rows and columns of figures on her computer screen and they were not telling her a happy story. Since the beginning of the heatwave, the animal-feed bills had gone up, as all the grazing on the farm had disappeared. Meanwhile the number of people visiting Silver Street Farm, and paying their entrance money, had gone down – it was just too hot to do anything.

Silver Street Farm was in trouble.

Just as Flora was thinking about exactly how *much* trouble they were in, the phone rang. It was someone from the Lonchester City Water Board. Did Miss MacDonald realize that Silver Street Farm was using twenty times more water this month than last month, and that there was a huge bill to pay? Flora was shocked.

"We can't be using twenty times as much!"

"I'm afraid so," said the lady on the phone. "And if this bill isn't settled within a month, we'll have to cut off your water."

Flora was about to explain that if the water was cut off then the Silver Street animals would die of thirst, when there was a sudden interruption: water gushing out over the office floor! Miss MacDonald ended her call rather quickly and ran outside, colliding with the children who had been filling their buckets from the tap under the office window.

"I've got to turn the water off at the mains!" exclaimed Flora as she rushed past. "Misty's chewed through the pipe under the sink *again*!"

It took less than a minute to stop the flood, but that was plenty of time for a lot of water to escape. Flora and the Silver Streeters stood in the office together and surveyed the damage. Pools of water covered the kitchen floor and the two old sofas, used for resting by the fire on cold days, stood in huge puddles of water. The rug between them was soaked and the computer was making a funny fizzing sound.

Standing in the middle of the biggest

puddle was the culprit: Misty the dog, his grey fur spiky with wet and a bit of blue plastic water pipe held triumphantly in his jaws.

"Look at him," said Meera. "He's *pleased*."

Meera was right. Misty's eyes sparkled with pleasure and his tail wagged steadily back and forth. It was clear that he thought he had done something really clever.

"He's always pleased when he chews through that water pipe," said Flora wearily.

"Tell him off, Flinty!" Karl said to Flora's sheepdog, who stood quietly at her side as always. "He's your puppy!"

"She's too much of a softie!" said Gemma.

"And it's too late to tell him off now anyway," said Flora. "You have to tell a dog off when it's doing the bad thing; afterwards is no good."

"He's chewed through that pipe four times now. Why?" Meera wondered.

"Who knows?" said Karl, "Come on Meera. Let's get mopping."

Meera took the mop and began to work, but she didn't stop wondering. There had to be a *reason* for it.

When the water had been mopped up and the pipe mended, Flora called a meeting and she and the children sat down in the yard with a large packet of biscuits. Flinty and Misty flopped in the shade by the office door, and the pup's dad, Buster the guard dog, jumped up from his post by the Silver Street gates and came to join the humans; biscuit crumbs were Buster's favourite and he was willing to put up with hot sun on his black coat to get them.

"OK," said Flora, after a mouthful of chocolate digestive, "I'll be straight with you all. We're in trouble. What we need is—"

"Some shade for the animals…" interrupted Meera.

"and for the visitors…" Gemma chipped in.

"…some fresh, green grass…" said Karl.

"OK," Flora continued, "what we *also* need is a *lot* more visitors and a supply of water that doesn't cost us anything. What we need is a Silver Street Survival Plan. Any ideas, guys?"

Biscuits crunched in the silence.

"Well," said Flora, "I'm going to turn my hand to ice-cream making. Let's see if a wee bit of homemade goats' milk ice cream pulls in the visitors. And tomorrow I'm going to start setting up some water tanks, so that when it *does* rain we can store it and I won't have to beg the Water Board for mercy … like I'm going to do now. You kids get off home. I'll be in trouble if you're late. And get your thinking caps on!"

Ten minutes later, Meera, Karl and Gemma were standing at a busy crossroads where their routes home went in different directions, reluctant to say goodbye.

"Flora's really worried," said Meera

"I don't blame her, after what we overheard her saying to the Water Board," said Gemma.

"We *have* had fewer visitors since this heatwave began," said Karl.

The children looked grim and studied the pavement in silence. As usual, it was Meera who cheered them up.

"OK, Silver Streeters," she announced, "here's your challenge! The person who comes up with the best way to find green pastures and water fountains to save our farm, wins…" Meera rummaged in her backpack and pulled out a sweet packet "a famous, magic green jelly baby!"

Gemma and Karl groaned and hit Meera over the head with their bags. But at least, for a moment, everyone was smiling.

Chapter Three

5.50 p.m. Flat 87a, Montague Heights

As Karl ate his tea, he stared out of the kitchen window, down over the rooftops spread out far below his home on the fifteenth floor.

"Karl, you are quiet," said Auntie Nat, peering at him across the table. "Why so quiet? Is first day of holidays, should be big cebrelation."

Auntie Nat had lived in Lonchester for years, at least for all of Karl's life, but she still had a strong Russian accent and sometimes got her words in a muddle.

"*Celebration,* Auntie," said Karl, biting another fish finger in two.

"Cebrelation, yes. That's right. So, why so quiet, eh?"

"Silver Street Farm's in trouble. There's no grass for the animals and no shade. They're getting too hot. And now we're running out of money for food and water, because it's *so* hot that people don't want to come and visit."

"It will rain soon," said Auntie Nat calmly. "Don't worry."

"I don't think it will," said Karl. "Just look at that sky – it's so blue!"

"Trust me, Karl," Auntie Nat answered, scooping up a forkful of peas. "The stars say very clear, rain next week. So soon, no problems."

Sometimes, Auntie Nat's faith in horoscopes drove Karl bonkers; he took a very deep breath and stared out of the window at the city below. Somewhere, down amongst all those tower blocks and office buildings, all those flyovers and bypasses and housing estates, there must be little patches of green grass that weren't brown and dry, that the Silver Street animals could enjoy. If only he could find them. If only he could *fly* over the city and *look* for them.

5.55 p.m. Lonchester City Museum Café

Meera's three little brothers were eating burgers shaped like dinosaurs in the museum canteen. Sadar, her littlest brother, had spread tomato ketchup all over his face and Mrs Gupta was trying to wipe it off. Sadar, meanwhile, was doing his best to bash their middle brother,

Dayal, with a rubber Hadrosaur from the museum shop.

"Come on, boys," said Mr Gupta. "The Dino Trail is starting in two minutes."

Meera rolled her eyes. Dinosaurs were so boring, they should all be called "Dullasaurs" as far as she was concerned. If she ate her chips *really* slowly, maybe they'd just let her wait here in the canteen. But Meera's oldest brother, Etash, was determined to share his love of dinosaurs with his big sister. He grabbed her hand and pulled her out of her chair.

"Come see dinosaurs!" he insisted.

"Oh, all right," Meera said, and let him lead her down the corridor towards the giant skeletons. How was she going to come up with a Silver Street Survival Plan with nothing but Diplodocus bones for inspiration?

* * *

6 p.m. 127 Woodbury Road, Lonchester

"Everybody ready to go?" Gemma's mother turned round in the passenger seat of the car and beamed, rather too brightly, into the back seat, where Gemma and her older brother Kevin sat side by side, scowling.

"S'pose so," mumbled Gemma.

"Oh, Mum," Kevin whined. "Do I have to come?"

"You do if you want driving lessons, young man," Gemma's dad chipped in sternly. "Now, let's just get on with this, shall we?"

It seemed to Gemma that Dad was just about as keen on the idea of a family as she and Kevin. Only Mum was trying to be cheerful about it, smiling like someone off a toothpaste advert.

"Right," said Mrs Woods brightly. "I'll read you what it says in the book!" She waved a book called *Ten Circular Walks in Lonchester.* "Circular walk number three," she read aloud. "The 'Barges and Bridges' walk will take you around a little-known section of the city canal."

"Great!" hissed Kevin from the back seat. "Walking in circles round some stagnant water."

Gemma bit into one of her plaits so she didn't have to show Kevin that he'd made her laugh.

6.15 p.m. Lonchester City Museum, Dino Trail

"Grrrrrrroooow!" said the huge model Tyrannosaurus rex, gnashing its giant, bloodstained teeth.

"Oooooeeeeeee!" squealed Meera's three little brothers, squirming with fear and delight.

"Well!" said Mrs Gupta, taking her husband's arm and stepping back a little. "It's certainly very lifelike!"

Yeah, thought Meera grumpily. *About as lifelike as plastic roses.* Whilst the T. Rex did some more gnashing, Meera went looking for something – anything – to make her less bored. It was good to get away from the crowds of overexcited tots and the artificial growling of long-extinct reptiles.

Meera wandered out of the animal section of the museum and into another where there were cabinets of old cups and plates, teapots and bottles.

"I don't believe it!" Meera breathed. "Something even *more* boring than dinosaurs!" In fact, it was so dull it was almost interesting! She stopped to check her reflection in the glass of one of the cabinets, but something apart from her own round face and big dark eyes caught her attention. Inside the cabinet were weird little bottles that looked like someone's pottery project gone wrong. Each one had the outline of an owl on the side, like some sort of advertising logo. "Roman Bottles from the Spring of Minerva, Lonchester," said the label. "The owl on the bottles symbolizes the Goddess Minerva, who was said to prevent the sacred waters of the sacred spring from ever running dry."

Wow! thought Meera. *That's what Silver Street needs – a spring that never runs dry!*

"The original site of the spring has been lost," she read on, "but evidence suggests that it may have been under what became the railway and the canal district of modern Lonchester. See map." Meera pressed her nose to the glass to examine the map and her heart began to race. There, right smack in the middle of the faded circle that marked where the Spring of Minerva might once have been, was ... Silver Street Farm!

6.35 p.m. Canal Walk, East Lonchester

Circular walk number three followed a particularly nasty bit of canal – a little dead end backwater that used to allow canal boats to deliver to the old abandoned factories that stood all around. Gemma thought it was dismal, but Kevin decided that it would be good for his art project. He got out a tiny video camera that he'd borrowed from school and began taking shots of something floating in the oily water.

"Yuck!" said Gemma. "I don't even want to know what that is."

"Dead rat, I should think," said Kevin.

Gemma walked off, looking for something nicer than dead rats.

There was at least a bit of green by the canal. She looked at the bushes and patches of grass on the far bank and as she looked a very pretty little black-and-white goat pushed its head out of a bush. While she was looking at the goat, Gemma noticed that, tucked in the shadows under the bank, was an old canal boat, long, narrow and black as coal. One end of the boat had a roof, a door, windows and a small chimney poking out, from which a little thread of smoke was escaping. The goat jumped from the bank and landed on the empty deck. Immediately the door flew open and a skinny lady with spiky black hair poked out her head.

"You done then, Flower?" she said to the goat. "Right, then. Off we go."

A moment later, the boat began to chug away down the canal and Gemma felt an idea for the Silver Street Survival Plan pop in her head like a bursting bubble. "Wait!" she called, running down the path after the boat. "Please wait!"

Kevin turned off his camera and looked after his sister.

"She's finally lost it!" he said to himself. "Always knew she would!"

6.45 p.m. Henleaze Park, Lonchester

As Karl was gazing *down* from his kitchen window, Bish Bosh was looking *up*. He too was thinking about flying.

Bish Bosh had come to Silver Street Farm

as a turkey thief, had become a regular helper and was now the foster parent of a goose. He'd been the first thing in the world that the goose had seen when she'd hatched in the Silver Street incubator and since that moment she'd followed Bish Bosh everywhere. At first, she'd been so tiny that it was hard for her to keep up with even the slowest walk. But now, she'd swapped her baby fluff for a suit of smooth, coffee-coloured feathers. She'd grown big too, "almost swan sized" as Bish Bosh was fond of saying. She was certainly as graceful as a swan, except when she hurried after Bish Bosh, waddling on her big webbed feet to follow his every move. Bish Bosh tried to pretend that having the goose as his shadow was a nuisance, but it was plain to see that he loved her.

She was a Canada goose, not a farmyard

bird, so he'd given her a special name as a reminder of where her ancestors came from: Chinook.

"I looked it up in a book," he had told Flora proudly. "It's a Native American word. The Chinook is 'the wind that brings the spring'."

Chinook certainly seemed to have brought some spring to Bish Bosh's life. Sergeant Short of the Lonchester police force, and a special friend of Silver Street, never had to call by any more to tell Flora that Bish Bosh was "in a bit of trouble". Even Squirt, his little brother, had noticed a difference. "He doesn't bash me half as much since he got that bird," he said. "And he smiles more."

Bish Bosh was smiling now as he cycled his bike in the park near where he lived. Finally, after days of pedalling away from the goose to try to encourage her to fly, not just walk, Chinook had at last spread her wings to follow him. He smiled up at her as she flew above him.

And Chinook, in her heart, smiled back.

12 midnight, Silver Street Farm

For all of Misty's short life, water had been hiding. Once, when he was very small and his brothers and sisters had still lived at Silver Street, water had come out of the sky in little drops. But almost at once it had hidden itself, sinking into the ground, out of sight and smell. Water liked to keep itself secret, always going inside and underneath, where you couldn't get it.

Misty knew that water was important; he knew that everything – every animal and every plant – at Silver Street was crying out for

it. So it was important to find water and make it come out of its secret, hidden places. He kept his ears open for water all the time, because water always *talked*.

Misty lay in the middle of the yard in the warm, dark night, his fluffy head resting on his paws. Sirens wailed, cars revved, humans laughed and screamed in the city around him, but there was only one voice he was listening to, tiny and buried beneath his two front feet.

Chapter Four

When the children arrived back at Silver Street Farm the next morning, they could see that Flora had been very busy indeed. The collection of old oil drums that had been lying about the farm had been turned into water butts and there was now one standing at the corner of almost every building, ready to catch the rain from the roof gutters.

"If it ever *does* rain again," said Flora as she disappeared into the dairy, saying she was not to be disturbed.

"Oh," said Gemma. "I wanted to tell her about my idea."

"Mmm," said Karl. "I did, too."

Meera looked at her friends. What would they say to a plan that involved digging up the farmyard in search of an ancient Roman fountain? An idea that had seemed so real and exciting in the museum now seemed completely mad. Meera found herself blushing just thinking about it.

"Don't forget about the magic green jelly baby," Meera said, to cover her embarrassment. "Tell *me* about your plans!"

Gemma had borrowed her brother's little video camera to show them the barge, its skinny, spiky-haired owner – who was called Pixie – and its nomadic goat, Flower.

"Yeah, I'll take your sheep and goats on board!" Pixie said to the camera, her earrings jangling and Flower bleating as she spoke.

"With Pixie's barge," Gemma explained, "we can move the animals to find grazing without having to worry about crossing roads!" Gemma's ginger plaits always danced about when she was especially excited about something, and they were doing that now.

Karl's plan was to find places where there was grass and the animals could graze. He'd brought a map of the city to help.

Meera saw at once that the *two* plans were really *one*. Karl's plan could *find* grass for the animals to eat and Gemma's could *take* the animals to it.

"Trouble is," said Karl, pushing his dark fringe out of his eyes, "you can't tell from a map if there's actually any grass growing at these spots, and if it's *still* growing after all the heat. What we need," he added, "is to be able to fly over the canal and look for green patches either side of it!"

Meera nudged her two friends, "Wow!" she said. "Talking of flying… *Look!*"

Cycling down the road towards the Silver Street gates was Bish Bosh, with his little brother Squirt sitting on the back of the bike. Meera had always liked how similar they were; identical fuzzy blonde heads, identical legs that were as knobbly as grass stalks, just two different sizes: long (Bish Bosh) and short (Squirt). Above them, flapping and gliding to match their speed, was Chinook.

The three friends watched, entranced, as Bish Bosh parked his bike and Chinook settled delicately beside him. She folded her wings and greeted the children goose fashion, by dipping her long neck and making "peep, peep, peep" noises. Buster got up from his post by the gate to wag his tail at Bish Bosh, and Chinook hissed at him. She didn't like dogs.

"Wotcha, guys!" said Bish Bosh and Squirt together.

"How long has she been flying?" asked Gemma.

"Since yesterday!" said Bish Bosh, unable to hide his pride.

"Wicked, isn't it?" said Squirt. "Can I show them, Bish Bosh? Can I?"

"Yeah, go on then," said Bish Bosh.

Squirt crouched down next to the bird

and gently felt under her feathers. He pulled out a tiny harness, unclipped it and held it up. Attached to the harness was a small pouch with a chocolate bar inside.

"She carried it all the way here!" said Squirt, beaming.

"Yeah, well," said Bish Bosh, grabbing the bar from Squirt's hand. "Chocolate, anyone?"

Meera looked at the pouch and the harness and then at the tiny camera in Gemma's hands, and the missing piece of the plan fell neatly into place.

Chapter Five

"Eye lykit ump 'eeer," Squirt said to Meera as they stood at the door of the old signal box and looked out onto the farm below.

"Take your face mask off, Squirt." Meera laughed. "We've finished cleaning out the chickens now, so you don't need it on any more."

"Ohmmph!" said Squirt. He pulled off the mask. "I said, I like it up here."

"Yeah, I do too."

They were quiet for a moment, looking out over the farm. Everything lay still in the heat. Well, almost everything.

"What *is* that silly dog doing?" asked Meera.

"Which silly dog? We've got three." Squirt grinned.

"Misty. Look at him," said Meera. Flinty's pup was pacing round and round the very centre of the farmyard, stopping every few seconds to scrabble at the concrete surface with his paws.

"He's a loony!" said Squirt.

"Maybe," said Meera uncertainly.

Meera watched Misty pace and dig, pace and dig. Could a dog know about a Roman spring, she wondered? But before she even had time to tell herself what a silly idea that was, Auntie Nat's big white van bounced over the bumps into the yard.

"That's torn it!" said Meera. "We'll a…
trouble if she finds out that Karl and the oth…
aren't here. We'd better get down there."

"Karl is where?" said Auntie Nat, sounding a little worried. All the children who helped at Silver Street were given strict instructions that they were to stay on the farm, where Flora could keep an eye on them, and come straight home when work was finished.

"I don't know," said Squirt before Meera had time to stop him. "He's gone on a wild-goose chase with my brother and Gemma." He laughed and Meera glared at him.

"Wild-goose chase? I don't understand."

"Oh, you know – escaping animals!" Meera chipped in quickly. "They've just popped through a fence to get a goose…" She waved vaguely in the direction of the turkey pen. At that moment Flora emerged from the dairy.

"Hello, Mrs Lebedeva!" said Flora.

Flora was so good at looking totally in control, even when she had no idea what was going on, that Auntie Nat relaxed and smiled.

"I understand you have escaping goose, yes?" Auntie Nat said, playfully waggling her finger at Flora. Behind Karl's auntie's back, Meera nodded vigorously at Flora, who was giving her a "what-is-going-on?" look.

"Oh, yes." Flora laughed nervously. "Now, what can we do for you?"

"*I* can do for *you*!" said Auntie Nat. "Look!" she said and threw open the back doors of her van proudly. "I have shade for animals and visitors!"

The van was packed with huge, brightly-coloured umbrellas. Squirt and Meera looked at each other mystified, but Flora seemed very pleased.

"Sunshades!" she exclaimed. "Where did you get them?"

"Nnnnn." Auntie Nat shrugged; she was always buying and selling things, but she liked to keep her deals a secret. "I know many people," she said mysteriously.

There were twenty orange, yellow and pink umbrellas and their heavy concrete bases to unload. Afterwards, Flora waved Auntie Nat off, promising that Karl would be home by five. But when Auntie Nat's van was out of sight, she turned to Meera and Squirt with a face like a thundercloud.

"So?" she said, her hands on her hips, and her blue eyes blazing. "Where are the others?"

Meera thought of some excuses, but they were all pretty lame. Squirt just shifted from one foot to the other. In the middle of the yard, the pup began to pace and scratch again.

"Lie down!" Flora ordered, and he instantly dropped flat in the shade beside his mother.

Meera was just wishing that she could do the same as Misty, when they heard the shouts of three cyclists tearing at top speed through the gates.

"I'm hoping," said Flora, her Scots accent making her sound especially stern, "that there's a *very* good explanation for all of this."

Chapter Six

Inside the office, the three dogs settled down on the rug and Chinook sat down on a cushion. Animals knew that when humans came in here, it was usually a while before they went out again.

The children plugged Kevin's camera into Flora's computer and waited anxiously for the data to download. The video was a bit wobbly at times and some of Chinook's feathers got in the way, but most of the time it gave a clear view of the area either side of the canal from

Silver Street down to where the canal met the river a few kilometres away.

"So," said Flora, "let me get this straight. You strapped the video camera to the goose and then got her to follow you?"

The children nodded.

"Why?"

"*That's* why," said Karl, pointing to a patch of green, lush grass on the video. "So we can see where there's grazing near the canal for the sheep and goats."

"And then we can put the animals on the barge and take them there," added Gemma.

"What barge?" said Flora.

It took a while to explain the whole plan to Flora and even after they had persuaded her to call Pixie on her mobile, she didn't seem completely convinced. At last she said, "I think this whole idea is completely crazy, but there's a chance – just a chance – that it could work. I need to think about it. OK?"

The children nodded.

"And," Flora continued, "I don't want anyone off the site without telling me first. You know the deal: when you're here, you stay here. Clear?"

Flora looked so stern that even Bish Bosh joined in with the reply.

"Clear, Flora," they all said.

"And now," Flora said, smiling for the first time in what seemed like ages, "while I think of it, I have two jobs for you. Job one: mend the sunshades and move them into the pens. Job two: ice-cream sampling!"

The animals loved their sunshades. Gemma and Meera put two of them into the sheep pen and Bobo and Bitzi moved from the cramped little patch of shade under the bramble bush and spread out in their new round pools of coolness. Their lambs had room to run around a bit, out of the sunshine. Even Zelda and Arkady, who hadn't seemed at all bothered by the heat, enjoyed the shade. Gemma tied the goats' hay net under one of the umbrellas so that they could eat and stay cool. Soon, every single pen had a bright sunshade umbrella.

The farmyard also got a little makeover. Auntie Nat had brought so many umbrellas that there were enough to put them all over the yard.

"It looks like a cafe!" said Karl.

"Well, we *are* eating ice cream!" said Meera. "Yum!"

Bish Bosh and Squirt didn't say anything –

they were too busy working at job number two.

"Well," said Flora, sucking her spoon thoughtfully, "even though I do say so myself, this ice-cream *is* good. I'm going to advertise it on the website and put up some pictures of our new sunshades. Hopefully that'll attract a few more visitors this Saturday. Goodness knows we need them..."

"And have you decided about our plan?" asked Gemma quietly.

"I still think it's madness. Sheep and goats on a barge, chugging up and down the canal! Crazy!" Flora shook her head. "But ... I think it might just work. So yes, you can go ahead tomorrow, if you like!"

"Yes!" said Bish Bosh and Squirt together; Karl and Gemma slapped palms.

"Don't get too excited," said Flora. "I've

still got to find a way to pay the Water Board *and* find a cheaper source of water."

Meera thought about the red circle on the museum map, about the spring that never ran dry and she opened her mouth to speak. But before she could say anything, Misty was pacing and scrabbling in the middle of the yard again, and everyone was telling him to stop.

"Whatever's got into that dog?" said Flora. "I think he's going barmy with the heat."

Maybe I am too, Meera thought. *I must be mad, to think that an ancient Roman fountain is under this place!*

Chapter Seven

Bobo liked the new shade thingies. At least now she didn't have to spend all of the hottest hours of the day scrunched up with her lambs. They had grown so big and demanding that, she was completely fed up with suckling them. Early mornings were the only time she got any peace, when it was still cool enough to wander about her pen and get away from them.

"Baaa!" said one of her lambs.

"Beeehhh!" said another one.

Bobo ignored them. She walked to the fence that ran along the edge of the canal and looked out over the water.

Something was happening. *Nothing* had been happening for so long that Bobo was almost shocked. Her heart beat faster; she pricked her ears forward and balanced her little front hooves on a lump of earth to stretch just a bit higher.

A large creature was coming towards Bobo, floating on top of the water as ducks did. On the back of the large creature was a human with dark wool on its head and a nasty goat standing beside it. The creature, the human and the smelly goat sailed right past her and Bobo was so absorbed in looking at this amazing sight that she didn't notice that her two lambs had ambushed her and were butting her udders in a very disrespectful way!

It was definitely time for weaning. Bobo stepped smartly away from the lambs and left them bleating.

All five Silver Streeters were waiting with Flora and the three dogs when Pixie's barge drew up to the wharf. Once, this was where cargo had been loaded on and off canal boats and onto the trains at Silver Street Station. It had been decided that the children would accompany the animals on their voyage as herding the animals and stopping them from escaping was a big job. Meanwhile, Flora would do the farm chores alone.

Pixie greeted them all with a wave. Although the barge was dark and rather drab-looking, Pixie herself was not. Her long skinny body was wrapped in layers of bright clothing, kaftans, scarves and bandanas. Her ears were pierced many times over and she wore a whole jewellery shop of odd earrings and silver bangles.All sorts of notes and numbers were written on her hands in blue biro. She seemed so bendy and fluttery that Meera found herself thinking of an exotic flag, waving in the breeze.

"This is very kind of you," Flora called out to her.

Pixie shook her head and, with it, her whole willowy body.

"No," she said. "It's not kind. I'm just bored of my own company." She grinned and the Silver Streeters found that her grin was infectious. They just had to join in.

Pixie *looked* a bit dippy, but when it came to handling her boat and getting the animals on board, she was as smart as a naval captain. She had what she called a "gangplank" – a sort of moveable walkway with a little rail either side, which was soon rigged up to run from the wharf to the deck of her barge. She'd even covered the gangplank in sacking so that it wasn't slippery for hooved feet.

"I don't use it myself much," she explained. "But when Flower isn't feeling too sprightly, it gets her on and off for her dinner!"

Flower, Pixie's pretty little Toggenberg goat, was tethered by her head collar to a ring on the wall of Pixie's cabin.

"That's what we should do with your goats, tether 'em," said Pixie. "But down the other end. My Flower is non too sociable".

Pixie showed Flora where the Silver Street goats should be tied and the spot on the deck where the Silver Streeters could put a little pen for the sheep.

In no time at all, everything was ready for the Silver Street animals to come aboard. The baby goats were too bouncy to be led over the gangplank, so Gemma and Meera tucked one under each arm and carried them. The two nanny goats, Arkady and Zelda, had to be tempted up the gangplank by a bucket of food shaken just in front of them.

By the time the goats were safely tethered on deck it was already getting warm.

"We need to get this done before it gets any hotter," said Flora as they all walked to the sheep pen. "It's at times like this that I really, really wish Flinty could herd sheep like a sheepdog's supposed to and not just chickens."

In fact, Bobo seemed quite keen to get onto the barge. She trotted happily over the gang-plank, and the rest of her little flock followed.

“OK,” said Pixie. “All aboard?”

“All set!” said Flora, smiling. “Let me just take a picture for the website. Who knows, this may get us bit of publicity!”

Flora snapped the barge and its cargo of six goats, six sheep, six people and one goose, in the bright sun of another clear day, as it set off down the canal. The children waved, the goats bleated and Chinook honked and flapped her wings, caught up in the general excitement.

Bobo sniffed the air as the barge chug-chug-chugged along. Amongst the hot, dry smells of the city, her nose picked up the scent of something green and growing. It put her in such a good mood that she even allowed her lambs a small drink of milk.

Chapter Eight

Lonchester City FM's most famous DJ, Rockin' Roland Rogers, was having a break. He'd found a little patch of waste ground between the radio station and the canal. Roland was sure that no one else in the world knew about his scrap of wilderness; he lay down, stretched out on the patchy grass and closed his eyes. When he opened them again, he found three faces looking down at him.

"Baah!" said the first face.

"Meeek!" said the second.

"Peep, peep, peep!" said the third.

Roland sat up. His peaceful secret spot had been discovered! Invaded by goats, sheep, a goose, a whole load of kids and ... Roland couldn't believe his eyes...

"*Pixie*?" said Roland as the barge captain led her goat onto the grass. "Am I dreaming?"

"*Roly!*" Pixie almost dropped Flower's lead in surprise. "What are *you* doing here?"

"Having a little break!" Roland said, laughing. "More to the point, what are *you* doing here?"

"I'm grazing my goat," said Pixie, grinning. "Roland Rogers, meet my new mates: Meera, Karl, Gemma, Bish Bosh and Squirt. Oh, yeah ... and the one with feathers is Chinook!"

Everyone shook hands, except Chinook, who dipped her head and peeped.

"That's goose for 'pleased to meet you'," Bish Bosh explained.

"Wow!" said Meera. "You're Rockin' Roland Rogers!"

"You did a phone-in about us!" said Gemma excitedly.

"I did?" said Roland.

"We're from Silver Street Farm," Gemma said, starting to speak very fast indeed. "Remember? You got people to phone in to say if they wanted a city farm or not —"

"And they *did*," said Karl, too thrilled about actually meeting Rockin' Roland to remember to be shy. "And then loads of people turned up —"

"And," Meera interrupted, "we all marched

to Silver Street, and —"

Roland held up his hands and laughed. "Yeah, yeah. I remember, OK? But what are you doing *here*?"

"Well," said Pixie to the Silver Streeters, "let's find a bit of shade. Then we can tell Roland all about it."

Everyone sat down on the grass and talked. The children explained about the drought and the lack of grass for the animals and the falling visitor numbers. Roland laughed out loud when they told him how they'd found his secret spot by watching a video taken by a flying goose! Then Meera asked Roland what all the children wanted to ask, but didn't dare.

"How do you know Pixie?"

"We-eelll!" said Roland, with a big smile. "That, as they say, is another story. And right now, I need to make a little phone call. I can feel an outdoor broadcast coming on!"

Flora was in the dairy, making another batch of goats' milk ice-cream, with the radio on.

"And now, Rockin' Roland has phoned in with a special live trail for his Saturday Show," said the presenter.

"Citizens of Lonchester," said Rocking Roland in his special DJ voice, "I've got some young friends here who are going to tell you about my live outside broadcast that's coming up tomorrow, Saturday morning..."

There was a pause and some whispering, and somewhere in the background a sheep bleated. Flora switched off the electric whisk. She was sure that she recognized that bleat!

A chorus of voices that Flora knew very

well spoke together: "On Saturday from noon to three o'clock, Rockin' Roland Rogers will be broadcasting live from Silver Street Farm where there will be..."

There was another pause and brief whispering, then Gemma's voice said, "...lots of baby animals – lambs, piglets and kids – that's baby goats."

Bish Bosh's voice, sounding unusually quiet said, "There will be a very special goose..."

"...homemade goats' milk ice cream. Which I know is yummy 'cos I've had some," said Squirt's voice.

"And," said Meera's voice, "a long-lost Roman fountain!"

"Seeee you Saturday!" said Rockin' Roland.

A Roman fountain? Dear me! thought Flora. *Meera's gone as bonkers as that pup, Misty!*

Chapter Nine

From first thing on Saturday morning, Silver Street was a very busy place, as all the regular helpers got the farm ready for a rather special version of its weekly open day. Auntie Nat and Mrs Gupta were sorting out mountains of cakes and teacups in the kitchen; Mr Gupta and Mr Woods were arranging tables and chairs under the sunshades in the yard; Mr Khan was setting up the microphones and loudspeakers for the PA system; and Gemma's mum and brother were out in the car park, cutting back weeds.

Flora and the boys were doing all the usual farm chores, plus getting ice cream, cheese and eggs ready to sell, whilst Meera and Gemma set up a big blackboard outside Flora's office.

"I just don't know what got into me!" said Meera as she wrote the words Programme Of Events in pink chalk. "I mean, even if there *is* a Roman fountain under our yard, how could we have found it by this morning?"

"Don't worry about it, Meera," said Gemma. "No one's going to notice with all this lot going on!"

Gemma was right. The programme on the blackboard was pretty full:

10.30 a.m. Demonstration of goat milking by Fiona MacDonald (farm manager)

10.45 a.m. Guided tour of farm

11 a.m. – 3.30 p.m. Sale of farm produce,

also tea, cakes and biscuits

1 p.m. Mr Khan and his Jazz Men play popular jazz hits

11 a.m. Lonchester City FM's very own Roland Rogers rocks from Silver Street!

12 noon Gala Arrival of pedigree Silver Street sheep, by boat!

By 10 a.m. everyone at the farm was ready. The sheep, together with Bish Bosh, Squirt and Chinook, were aboard Pixie's barge prepared for their Gala Arrival at noon. Apart from Auntie Nat and Mrs Gupta, who were giggling away over the tea urn, everyone was calm.

By 11 a.m., all that calm had disappeared. Visitors thronged through the gates. Rockin' Roland's broadcast van was parked in the yard and the DJ was already getting the crowd very excited. Everyone was rushed off their feet. Most visitors were simply enjoying the animals and the sunshine, but there were a few problems: Karl had to pull two toddlers out of the pigs' mudbath, Meera managed to stop someone feeding the goats chewing gum just in time and Gemma caught a man trying to put a chicken into a carrier bag. In the kitchen, Auntie Nat was on her mobile phone, calling friends to bring emergency cake supplies as the ones she and Mrs Gupta had baked were disappearing fast.

It went on being so busy that Meera rather lost track of time and she didn't realize that the "Gala Arrival of Pedigree Silver Street sheep, by boat" was very overdue until she heard Rockin' Roland's announcement to the crowd.

"Real-life drama here at Silver Street," he said, sounding as if he really did care. "I've just heard that the barge, with the Silver Street

sheep and several precious humans aboard, has suffered engine failure!"

Bish Bosh and Squirt had had a wonderful morning riding up and down the canal in Pixie's barge. It was fun exploring the waterway and using Karl's map to find green spots for the sheep to graze. As they headed back, ready for the Gala Arrival, Pixie told them stories about touring the world with her band. She was just about to tell them how she first met Rockin' Roland, when there was a horrible jolt and the barge came to sudden stop.

Roland put on an extra-long record so they could discuss the crisis.

"I got a text from Pixie ten minutes ago, saying 'engine blown up' and now I can't get a reply." Roland ran his hands through his hair until it stood up on end. "They could be sinking!"

"Well, they won't sink far," said Flora. "I don't think the canal's more than a metre deep at the best of times."

"But we've still got to do *something*!"

"Sergeant Short!" said Meera. "He helped us out when the turkeys floated down the canal. Let's try him."

Meera borrowed Roland's mobile and dialled the sergeant's number. It was almost impossible to hear over the noise, so she blocked her other ear and closed her eyes. Roland and the others watched Meera's scrunched-up face anxiously for clues, but the moment she hung up, she beamed.

"You won't believe where he is!" Meera giggled. "He's on the canal, leading a canoe course for police cadets!"

* * *

Sergeant Short and his cadets were towing Pixie's barge with their canoes. He smiled to himself as he paddled the last few hundred metres towards the Silver Street Wharf. He could imagine what a sight they were making for the hundreds of people standing and cheering on the canal side.

"Are you a hero, Sergeant Short?" Bish Bosh called from the front of the barge.

"What do you reckon Bish Bosh?" said the sergeant.

"Dunno," Bish Bosh replied. "But Chinook likes you, look!'

Sergeant Short turned around as a goose landed on the deck of his canoe.

"Peep, peep peep!" Chinook said, dipping her long graceful neck under his arm.

Chapter Ten

It turned into one big party after that. Mr Khan and his Jazz Men began playing and everyone danced. Rockin' Roland twirled Pixie round and lifted her right off the ground.

Then, right in the middle of everyone having a brilliant time, a huge digger arrived at the Silver Street gates and a man in a yellow hard hat climbed down from the machine and stepped up to the microphone. The music stopped and everyone stood still.

"Ladies and gentlemen," said Hard Hat Man. "I'm afraid there's an enormous great leak in the water pipe under your feet and we have to dig an enormous great hole to fix it, *right now*."

People scrambled out of the way of the digger and watched as it took vast bites out of the concrete of the yard.

"Oh, dear," said Flora. "I really hope the Water Board will pay to fix all this damage."

Meera didn't say a word. Her heart was beating so fast and so loud she was sure everyone must be able to hear it. Was the Spring of Minerva about to be uncovered?

The digger stopped and the Hard Hat Man jumped down into the deep hole to take a look. Everyone crowded to the edge of the hole. There at the bottom was ... not an ancient Roman spring, but a massive metal pipe with an enormous hole in it.

"I think that's the cause of your huge water bills," said Hard Hat Man. "You certainly won't have to pay them when I report this."

He seemed rather surprised when Flora jumped into the hole and gave him a big hug.

Everyone was so busy looking down into the hole that they didn't notice the first drops of rain. Then people *did* notice and started looking up, smiling and laughing. The rain fell faster and people let it fall on their faces – they let it soak them to the skin! Water gurgled down the gutters into the water butts that Flora had set up.

"Another hour of this," said Flora, climbing out of the hole, "and Silver Street won't be thirsty for a very long time."

Only Meera still stared down at the broken

pipe. She had been so sure about the spring. Misty brushed against her leg. He licked her hand and wagged his tail. He'd known about the leak all along – just like Auntie Nat had known about the rain.

"Never mind, Meera," said Gemma as she and Karl came to stand beside their friend.

"The good thing," said Karl, "is that we won't be dug up by a whole load of archaeologists looking for Roman remains!"

"No," said Meera, starting to laugh. "The *really* good thing is that we have the world's only water-divining dog. And," she added with a huge grin, "Auntie Nat has saved a whole chocolate cake for us!"

Arm-in-arm, the Silver Streeters went inside, followed by one very happy dog and a flapping peeping goose.